Thomas Nelson and Sons Ltd
Nelson House Mayfield Road
Walton-on-Thames Surrey
KT12 5PL UK

51 York Place
Edinburgh
EH1 3JD UK

Thomas Nelson (Hong Kong) Ltd
Toppan Building 10/F
22A Westlands Road
Quarry Bay Hong Kong

Thomas Nelson Australia
102 Dodds Street
South Melbourne
Victoria 3205
Australia

Nelson Canada
1120 Birchmount Road
Scarborough Ontario
M1K 5G4 Canada

Letterland was devised by Lyn Wendon and is part of
the *Pictogram* system © Lyn Wendon 1973-1993

ISBN 0-17-410171-6
NPN 10 9 8 7 6 5 4 3 2

Printed in Italy

Naughty Nick and the Nettle Nibbler

Written by
Stephanie Laslett

Illustrated by
Jane Launchbury

Nelson

There was a large crowd around the Letterland noticeboard. Naughty Nick was nailing up a big notice. Everyone gathered near, craning their necks to see what it said.

"The Letterland Riding Races will be held next week," said Naughty Nick. "Anyone who wants to enter must write their name here — nice and clearly."

"I will enter on my ostrich," declared Oscar Orange.
"And I will ride my goat," giggled Golden Girl. Fireman Fred and Eddy Elephant decided to enter together. Soon the noticeboard was full of names.

The Letterland Riding Races were always held in one of Fireman Fred's fields. The next day everyone set off to practise — the Hairy Hat Man on his horse, Henry, Oscar on his ostrich, and so on. In fact, nearly everyone from Letterland was there. Even Quarrelsome Queen went along to watch.

But when they arrived to their dismay they found that the field was knee-deep in nettles. Nettles as far as the eye could see.

"Oh no!" said the Hairy Hat Man. "There's no way that we can have the Letterland Riding Races here."

"Nonsense!" snorted Quarrelsome Queen. "I'm not nervous of these nasty nettles! We can cut them down in no time!" But as soon as she tried, the leaves fell on top of her.

"Ow!" she shrieked, as a nettle landed on her nose. "This is horrible. No more nettles for me!"
"What a nuisance!" complained Fireman Fred. "How on earth can we get my field back to normal?"
"There's nothing we can do," sighed Poor Peter. "We'll never get rid of them in time."

Naughty Nick said nothing. He was too busy watching Doris the donkey.

She was nibbling the nettles just inside the gate. "Mmmm. Naughty ... but nice!" she said, licking her lips. Everyone turned to look.

"Now, Doris..." said Clever Cat. "If you were to nibble non-stop, day and night, could you eat all the nettles in this field by Sunday?"

The donkey nudged the nearest nettle with her nose. She gazed across the field, then slowly swung her head from side to side.

"No. No, I'm afraid not," she sighed. "But it would be nice to try," and she began to nibble again.

"This is no good," sniffed Poor Peter. "We're getting nowhere."
"Never mind!" shouted Naughty Nick. "Now I know what we need!" And he ran off at high speed back towards his house.

For the rest of that day nobody saw Naughty Nick. But they knew exactly where he was. The noise from his workshop was deafening.
"What a racket!" complained his neighbours. "What *is* he doing?"

Night-time came but there was still no end to the noise. The next morning there was a notice on the workshop door.

Nick's Workshop

"NO ENTRY!" it said. "To all my neighbours, near and far. Sorry about the noise, but I am working on a new invention. I know it is a nuisance … but it is necessary! PS. I need more nails!"

"What nonsense!" spluttered Sammy Snake. "This non-stop noise is giving me nightmares!" But there was still no sign of Naughty Nick.

Two days later the noise stopped. All was quiet and still. Kicking King called though the keyhole. "Naughty Nick! Are you in there?" But there was no answer.

*S*uddenly the doors flew open and a *new* noise started up. "Clanka, clanka, clink, clink," it went, and out through the doors came the strangest sight.

"Now you can see my new invention," announced Naughty Nick proudly. "Make way!"
He was sitting on top of an enormous wooden machine. It had four big wheels and, sticking out in front, NINE gnashing sets of teeth.

"Strong teeth! Just like Doris the donkey!" explained Naughty Nick. "But my machine eats nettles nine times as quickly!"

"It's marvellous!" exclaimed Munching Mike.
"It's super!" hissed Sammy Snake.
"It's FANTASTIC!" said Fireman Fred.
"It's nothing of the sort," replied Naughty Nick. "It's a Nettle Nibbler! Follow me!" and he set off down the road to the Race Field.

You could tell that the machine had been made by Naughty Nick because it was a little bit naughty itself!
It took a bite out of the Hairy Hat Man's hat. It chewed up one of Jumping Jim's juggling balls. It even bit a hole in Robber Red's sack!
"It's nearly as good at munching as me!" laughed Munching Mike.

S'oon they reached the field. Naughty Nick pulled a lever on top of the Nettle Nibbler. Everyone held their breath.
"Here goes," said Naughty Nick and he pushed a large red button marked 'NIBBLE NOW'.

Suddenly the nine sets of teeth began gnashing and nibbling through the nettles as if the machine hadn't eaten for months.
"Hooray!" cheered the crowd as the machine chomped its way across the field.

"Now we can have the Races after all," giggled Golden Girl.

S'ure enough, the Nettle Nibbler cleared the field in no time. It worked all morning and by the afternoon there was not a nettle to be seen.

"Well done, Naughty Nick," cried the Hairy Hat Man. "Let the Letterland Riding Races begin!"

Everyone lined up for the race to begin. Sammy Snake was the Race Starter.
"Ready, ssssteady, go!" he shouted and off they went, galloping down the field. Suddenly, from behind them all, came a strange noise.

"**C**lanka, clanka, clink, bonk!"
It was the Nettle Nibbler and
Naughty Nick! They streaked
down the field and crossed the Finish
Line just ahead of Oscar Orange.

Everyone cheered loudly and the
Hairy Hat Man cried, "Hooray, Oscar
Orange wins first prize! But we now
need a special prize for Nick and his
Nettle Nibbler, too."

Can you guess what prizes they got?
A shiny new hammer for Naughty
Nick and a net full of nettles for the
Nettle Nibbler, of course.

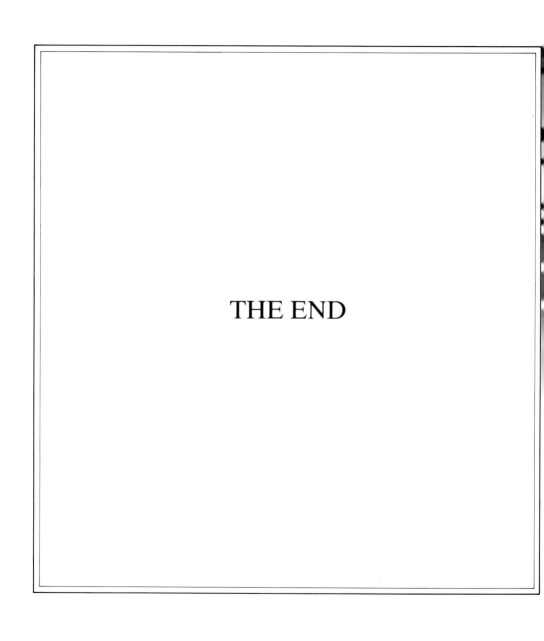

THE END